To Radley & Rhett,

Reading leads the way to greatness! ⭐

Alexandra ⭐
Adlawan

How I Spent My Summer Vacation

THE ADVENTURES OF MADDIE AND ALBERT

WRITTEN AND ILLUSTRATED BY ALEXANDRA ADLAWAN

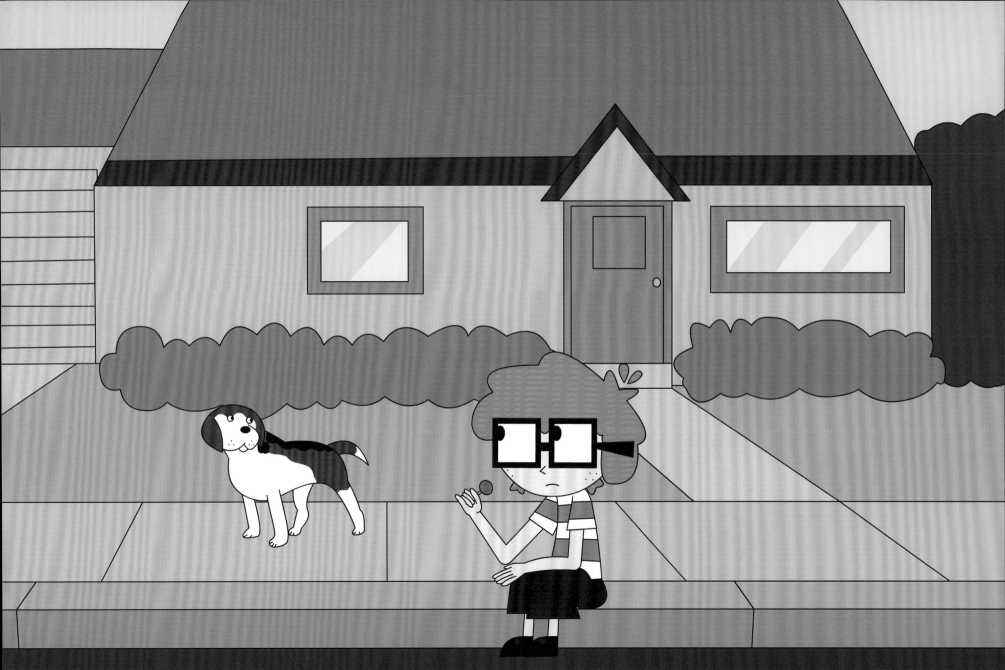

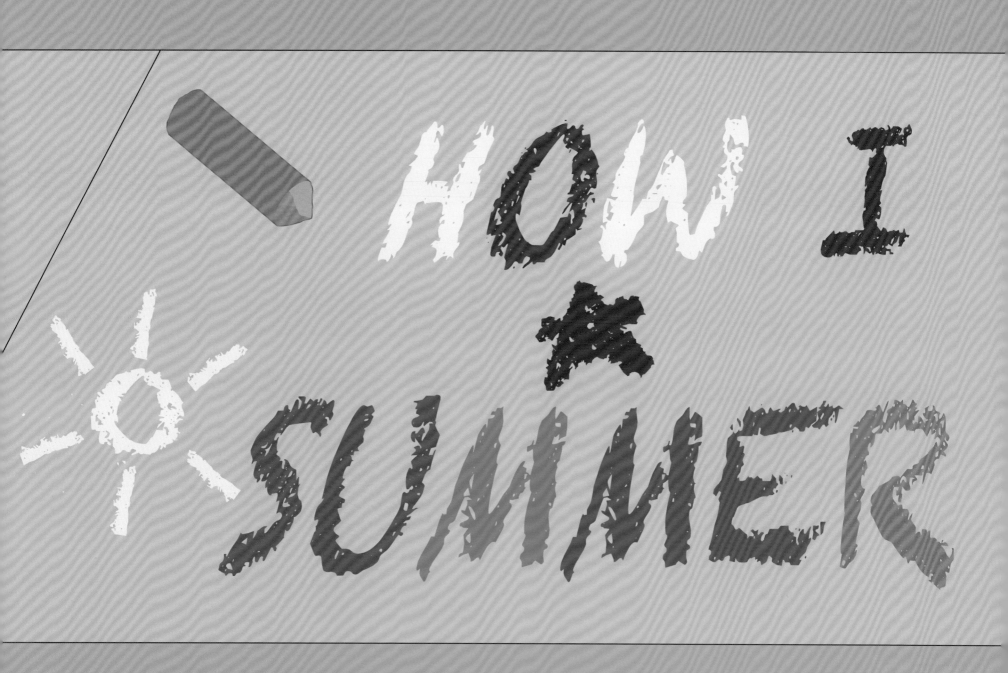

SPENT MY :)
VACATION

Went joyriding

Attempted to understand the laws of gravity

Looked for change
in the couch

Tried to give my beagle a bath

Made a life-size T-Rex out of popsicle sticks

Smashed a watermelon with a mallet

Learned to surf

Launched a
model rocket

Dug a hole to China

Tried to swing over the top of the swing set

Went mini golfing

Tried on hats

Went fishing

Attempted to fly

Painted a masterpiece

Cooked an egg on the sidewalk

And basically accomplished absolutely nothing!

Thanks to Mom and Dad for helping with my dream of sharing Maddie and Albert with the world. Tawd (pronounced: Todd), my mentor, your support and patience will always be close to my heart.

Alexandra Adlawan is an author/illustrator on the Autism Spectrum. In her first book "WILD IMAGINATION – THE ADVENTURES OF MADDIE AND ALBERT", we were introduced to these two lovable opposites who find a way to form a bond. In "HOW I SPENT MY SUMMER VACATION – THE ADVENTURES OF MADDIE AND ALBERT", these two goofballs continue to share with us their love of life and the joy of being best friends. Alexandra's goal in writing her books is to encourage the imagination within young people and to embrace the differences in others.

Across the Spectrum

FIRST EDITION 2019

ISBN 978-1-7324462-2-9

Library of Congress
Control Number: 2018913977

Printed and Bounded in China

Published by:
Amazing Artists LLC
2336 Heather Avenue, Long Beach, CA USA
www.amazingartists.online